Fierce Animals

Written by
David Orme

Some animals are fierce because they eat other animals.

They may have sharp claws and teeth.

Sometimes animals need to defend themselves. This makes them fierce.

Even pets can be fierce sometimes!

Bull shark

The bull shark is the fiercest of all the sharks.

Bull sharks even catch and eat other sharks!

It has the strongest bite of any sea animal.

Bull sharks can swim up rivers and attack animals and people.

Tiger

Tigers are the biggest wild cats in the world.

They attack animals at night for food.

They creep up on their prey very quietly.

When they are close enough, they jump on the animal.

Then they bite the animal's head or neck to kill it.

Polar bear

Polar bears are the biggest meat eaters that live on land.

They love eating seals!

Seals make holes in the ice. This is where they come up to breathe.

Look out! That polar bear is waiting!

Wolf

A wolf is a type of wild dog.

Wolves live and hunt together in a group called a pack.

Wolves are fast. They can run at 65 kilometres an hour.

When wolves work together, they can catch and kill large animals such as moose or caribou.

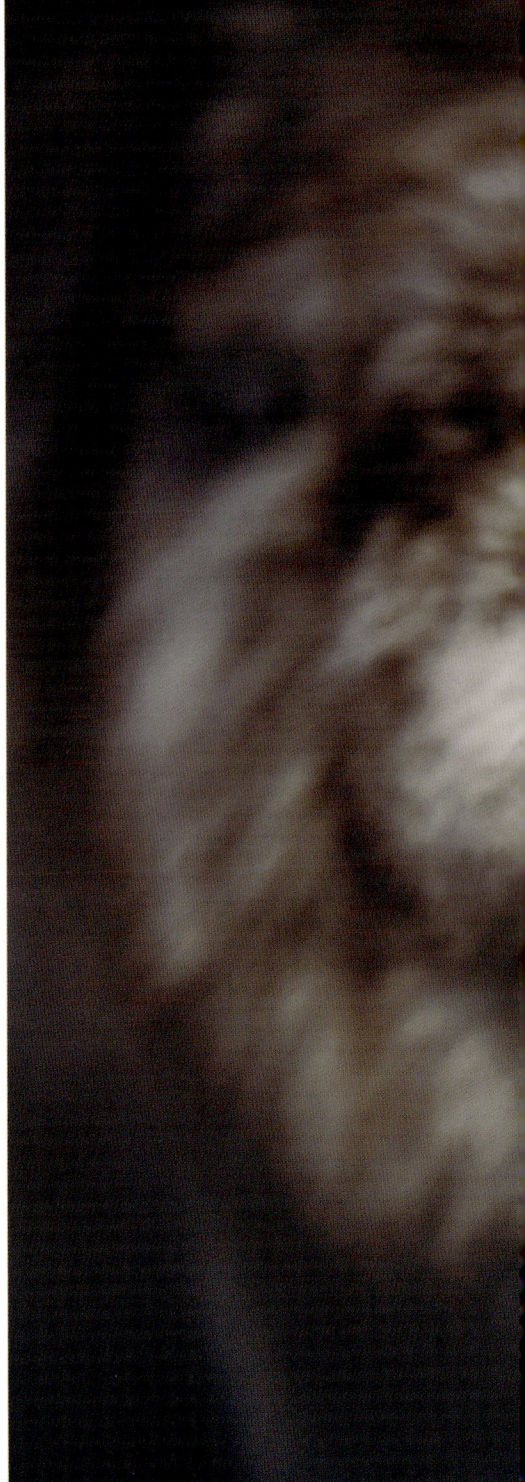

Crocodile

A crocodile is a type of animal called a reptile.

Crocodiles have sharp teeth and a very strong bite.

When a crocodile sees its prey, it can move very fast. Crocodiles eat fish, birds, and animals. Sometimes they eat people.

Doing this is a bad idea!

Honey badger

Honey badgers are found in Africa, Asia and India.

Take care! They are not at all friendly.

Honey badgers can even chase lions away and steal their food.

Some people think that honey badgers are the fiercest animals in the world.

The most dangerous creature

So what is the most dangerous creature in the world?

It is this one: the mosquito.

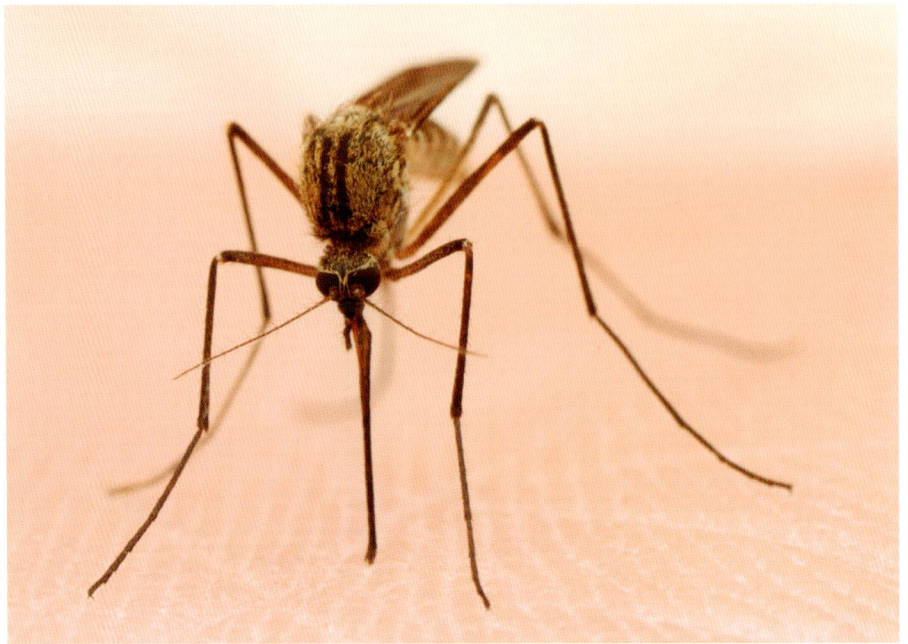

The mosquito is tiny, but it spreads disease. Every year it kills more people than any other creature.